The Trouble with with Normal

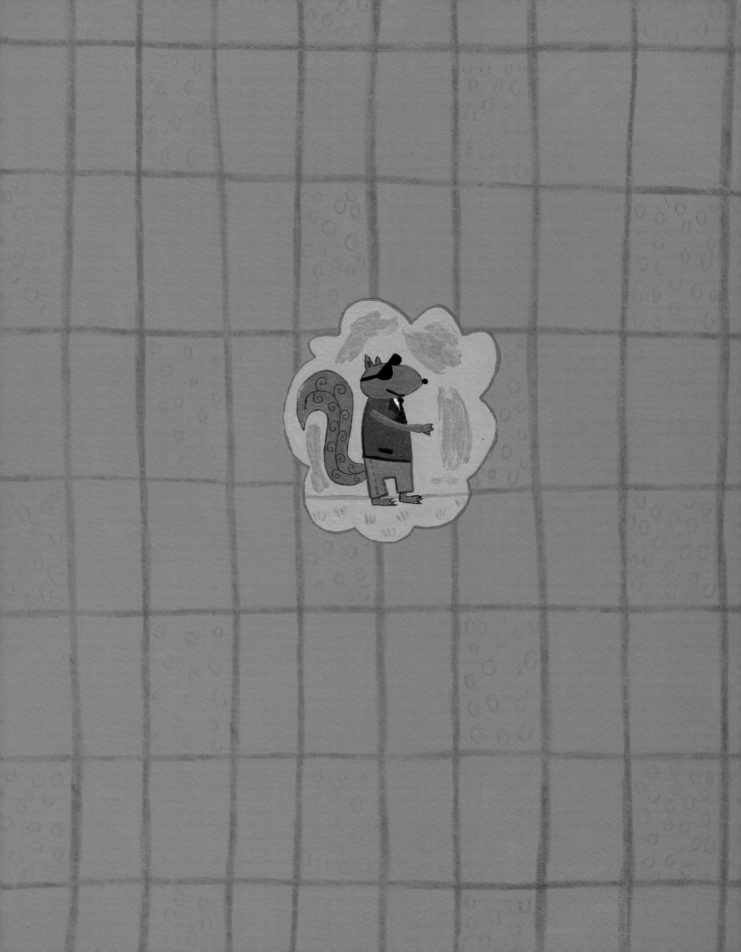

The Trouble with NORMAL

Charise Mericle Harper

Houghton Mifflin Company Boston 2003

WHO MOVED AWAY TO FOLLOW HER DREAMS.

FOR MY FRIEND RUTH

Copyright © 2003 by Charise Mericle Harper

www.houghtonmifflinbooks.com

The text of this book is set in Martin Gothic Medium.
The illustrations are acrylic with collage elements.

Library of Congress Cataloging-in-Publication Data
Harper, Charise Mericle.
The trouble with normal / written and illustrated by Charise Mericle Harper.
p. cm.
Summary: Finnigan, a Secret Service squirrel in training, reports
on the unusual activities in the apartment building across from his park.
ISBN 0-618-15626-7 (hardcover)
[1. Squirrels—Fiction. 2. Apartment houses—Fiction.] I. Title.
PZ7.H231323 Tr 2003   [Fic]—dc21   2002005088

Printed in Singapore
TWP 10 9 8 7 6 5 4 3 2 1

Me

FINNIGAN

This is a story about my friend Finnigan.

Finnigan is a squirrel and just about the best friend a boy could ever have. He's not like those ordinary squirrels that scamper around public parks and beg for nuts.

Finnigan is a squirrel of exceptional character.

1 He always tells the truth.*

2 He has a fantastic memory.

3 He notices new things.

AND

4 He wants to work for the president of the United States. Ever since I first met Finnigan he's dreamed of becoming a Secret Service squirrel.

squirrel

President

ESCAPE

SECRET SERVICE

NEWS

TOP DOG

DARK SUIT

AGENT OF THE WEEK

6 TIPS ON LOOKING

He said Secret Service agents wear dark glasses and are always on the lookout.

For his birthday I bought him a pair of sunglasses so he could practice

watching

I live at 1527 Walnut Street in a building called Normal Towers. Finnigan lives in the third walnut tree from the right in the park across the street.

Every night before I go to bed I stand in my window and turn my flashlight on and off 3 times. It's my secret good-night signal for Finnigan.

Finnigan says he always waves back, and even though it's too dark for me to see, I believe him.*

Finnigan did lots of practice-watching with his new glasses.
He was, after all, a Secret Service squirrel in training.

First he watched
my window,

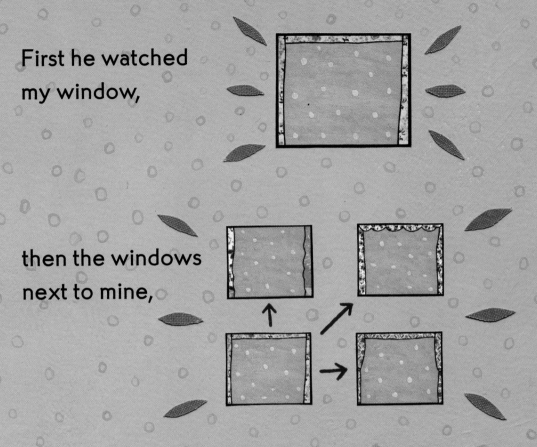

then the windows
next to mine,

and finally all the windows
in my building.

Finnigan said it was the duty of Secret Service agents to report suspicious activity. And he thought everyone in Normal Towers was acting awfully suspicious—that is, everyone except me—so he wrote a report.

He let me read it before he sent it off to the president in Washington.

The Trouble with Normal

A

REPORT

by

FINNIGAN

(Secret Service Squirrel in Training)

The following is a report of the suspicious activity taking place at 1527 Walnut Street.

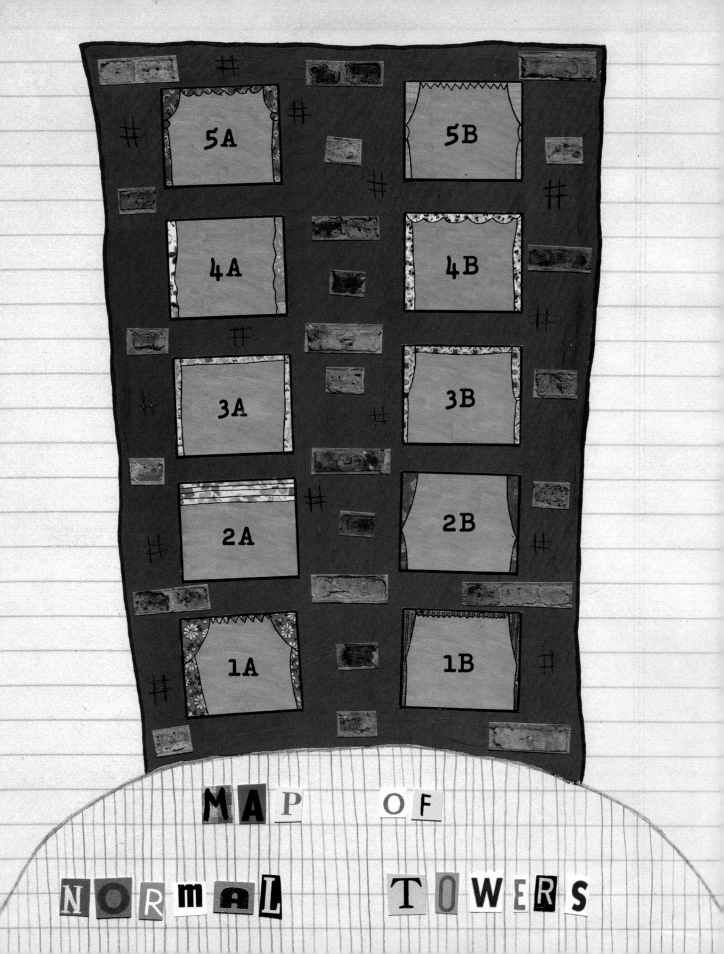

1A jumps up and down on his bed 6 times before going to sleep.

1B buys flowers for his pet bee.

2A performs sock puppet shows for his cat.

2B carves Halloween pumpkins all year long.

3A flashes flashlight on and off

3 times before going to bed.

3B always eats birthday cake

for dessert.

4A draws a picture of the sun on

her window when it is raining.

4B throws ball to dog in

apartment 5A.

5A catches ball from

apartment 4B.

5B wears a dish towel as a cape.

This is the end of my report.

Finnigan

Finnigan

I told Finnigan I thought the report was very professional. He said he was sure the president would send an agent down from Washington as soon as possible to help investigate. Then he said I shouldn't worry about my description in the report . . .

3A flashes flashlight on and off 3 times before going to bed.

. . . because he would explain everything to the agent.

SQUIRREL LUNCH

He couldn't leave me out, he said,
because Secret Service agents never lie.

All that summer Finnigan waited for a message from Washington. We played climbing and hiding games as usual, but I could tell he was distracted.

Then one morning when we weren't even thinking about it, a letter arrived. It was from the president.

Dear Mr. Finnigan,

Thank you very much for your fine report.
We have done some research and have
decided that there is no trouble with Normal.
In fact, the people of Normal are perfectly
normal. However, we were so impressed by
your work that we would like to invite you
to come to Washington to become an official
Secret Service squirrel. We need more
squirrels like you.

Signed,

The President of the United States

Finnigan could hardly believe it. Before I could say anything he was rushing around the park digging up all of his hidden nuts.

START

nuts

Soon his suitcases were packed and he was ready to go.
I was a little sad, because he seemed so happy to be
leaving. He promised that even though he was moving
away we'd still be friends.

ACTUAL SIZE

Then he handed me his lucky peanut.

I put it around my neck and promised never to forget him.

THOUGHTS OF FINNIGAN

MY PAL

Never

LUCKY PEANUT

He said he was going to be the best pen pal a boy could ever have. I walked with him to the edge of the park, then waved as he headed off to Washington.

He was a squirrel following his dreams.

I got my first postcard just the other day.

It has a picture of the White House on the front,

and this is the message on the back:

Of course I wrote him right back. I'm going to go and visit him in the spring, and if I'm lucky, maybe I'll even meet the president.

In the meantime, everything is still pretty much normal at Normal Towers. I don't flash my flashlight 3 times at night anymore, but sometimes I eat birthday cake for dessert.

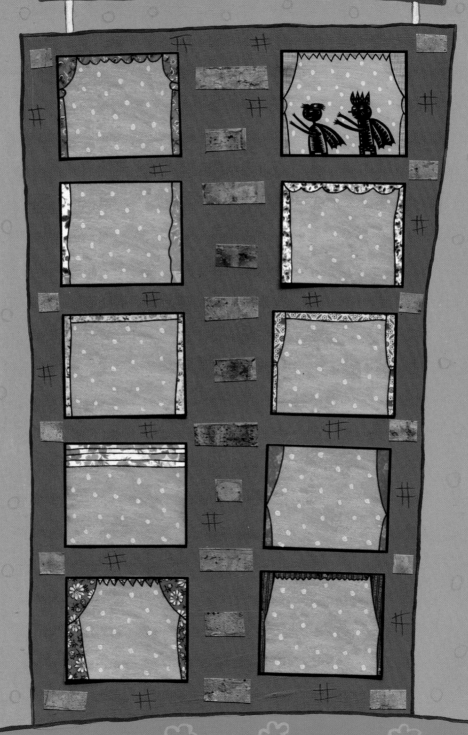

Or wear a dish towel as a cape.